minedition

English editions published 2017 by Michael Neugebauer Publishing Ltd., Hong Kong

Illustrations copyright © 2012 Nina Töwe

Rights arranged with "minedition" Rights and Licensing AG, Zurich, Switzerland.

Michael Neugebauer Publishing Ltd.,
Unit 28, 5/F, Metro Centre, Phase 2, No. 21 Lam Hing Street, Kowloon Bay, Kowloon, Hong Kong.
Phone +852 2807 1711, e-mail: info@minedition.com
This edition was printed in October 2016 at L.Rex Printing Co Ltd.
3/F., Blue Box Factory Building, 25 Hing Wo Street, Tin Wan, Aberdeen, Hong Kong, China
Typesetting in Goudy Old Style
Library of Congress Cataloging-in-Publication Data available upon request.

ISBN 978-988-8341-36-8

10 9 8 7 6 5 4 3 2 1 First impression

For more information please visit our website: www.minedition.com

Jack & the Beanstalk

A Folktale

Pictures by Nina Töwe

minedition

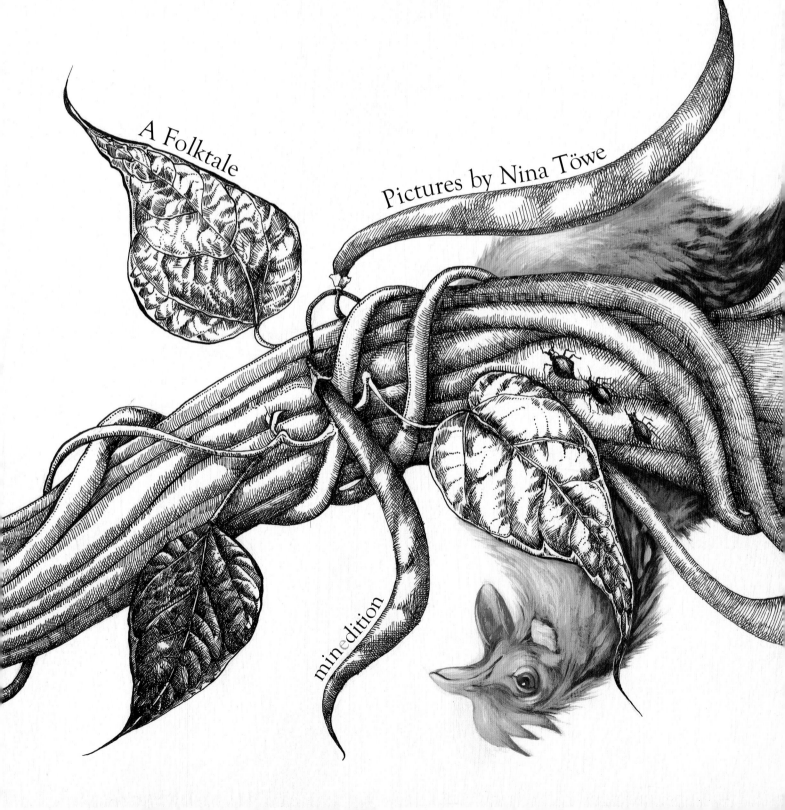

Once upon a time there lived a boy called Jack. He was a happy boy and his mother loved him very much. In fact, she gave him everything she could, until all they had left in the world was their little cottage and their faithful brown cow.

"Oh dear, Jack!" she cried one day, "what trouble we are in. Look in this cupboard!" Jack saw at once that there was nothing for them to eat.

"We have no choice my son," sobbed his mother, "we must sell the cow. As much as we love her, we must have food."

Jack comforted her and dried her tears. "Don't worry," he told her, "I will take care of it." And off he went, leading the brown cow.

He had not walked far, when he met a man coming the other way. "What a good looking cow you have there," he said admiringly.

"I'm taking her to market," replied Jack.

"Well, I can take her off your hands," smiled the man, "and I'll give you this bag of magic beans in return!"

"Magic?" asked Jack. "What's magic about them?" But the man was already leading the cow away down the lane. Jack looked at the beans, pale pink and speckled with little black dots. They looked quite ordinary to him.

And now he had to face his mother. Perhaps she would be pleased to have magic beans!

He hurried home, calling, "Mother, look what I've got!"

When she saw the beans, her mouth fell open with disbelief.
ou gave our lovely cow away for a handful of beans?"

"The man said they were magic, Mother!" exclaimed Jack.

"Magic?" she shrieked. "You idiot, now we have nothing!"
Vith that she knocked the beans from his hand
nd they fell down onto the earth.

When Jack woke up the next morning, there was a
strange green light in his room. He jumped out of bed
and ran to the window, and there he saw an amazing sight.
Outside the cottage, a huge leafy beanstalk had appeared.
When he rushed outside, he saw that the beanstalk towered
high up into the sky, so high he could not even see the top.

Hearing him outside, Jack's mother came into
the garden and could not believe her eyes.
"What on earth is happening?"
she whispered nervously.

"I don't know Mother, but I am going to see
what's at the top!" laughed Jack.
"No son, you will hurt yourself! Please stay here!"
she cried.
But it was too late, he was already almost as high
as the roof of their cottage, climbing quickly and
pulling himself up on the strong, broad leaves.
"Don't worry, I will find our fortune!"
he shouted down.

Jack climbed for a long time, until at last he
stepped off the beanstalk, and into a strange,
stony land. He was not sure how he would find
his fortune in this dull place. Then he saw an
old woman slowly hobbling towards him.

"Jack!" she called. "At last you're here!"
How strange, thought Jack, that she should know my name, and he
waited for her to speak again.

"Jack," said the old lady, "did your mother ever tell you how your
father died?"

Jack's eyes filled with tears. "I know that he died when I was only little."
"No, Jack," she replied, shaking her head sadly, "your father was killed
by a Giant, who took all that he had–his money, his precious things,
and put it in his castle!"

"Where is this Giant?" he asked, seething with rage.

"You must find him, before he finds you!" warned the
old woman, and with that, she disappeared.

Jack looked around him fearfully, not sure where to go. Then, far in the distance he could just see the outline of a great, dark castle far away. As he got nearer, he saw a woman sitting outside the gate. When she spotted him, she shouted, "Run away! Quickly, my husband will be home at any minute!"

But Jack was a brave boy. "Please, I am so thirsty, could you get me a drink?"

"Well, you must hurry. If my husband sees you, he will eat you at once!"

Inside the castle kitchen, Jack could see a huge cauldron bubbling on the fire, as the woman poured milk into a cup for him. Just as he finished drinking, there was a terrible roar at the gate of the castle:

"FEE, FIE, FO, FUM! I SMELL THE BLOOD OF AN ENGLISHMAN!"

The gate crashed open.

"Quickly!" whispered the woman, and she opened the cold oven door and Jack leapt inside. A second later, he felt the earth-shaking thud of the Giant's footsteps.

"BE HE ALIVE OR BE HE DEAD, I'LL GRIND HIS BONES TO MAKE MY BREAD!"

Jack held his breath and peeped through the hinges in the oven. The enormous Giant lumbered over to the table.

"Where's my supper, Wife? I'll get it from the oven!"

"No, no! Here it is!" and she tipped the cauldron up and filled his great bowl with food.

When the Giant had emptied the bowl and drunk a barrel of wine, he started to look quite drowsy. "Wife!" he roared, "Bring me my hen and then get to bed!"

The wife rushed in with a hen sitting in a straw basket. "Lay!" boomed the Giant.

Jack watched with astonishment as the hen laid an egg of pure gold each time the Giant ordered, "Lay!"

Soon the Giant began to fall asleep, nodding his head back in the chair.

Quietly, Jack opened the oven door and crept out. He crawled silently over to the table, lifted the basket and dashed from the kitchen and out of the great castle gates. He ran as fast as he could, over stones and around rocks until he saw the beanstalk, and scrambled all the way down, clutching the basket under one arm.

Jack's mother was overjoyed to see him, and so happy to see the magic hen who laid golden eggs. How good life was!

But Jack was still angry with the Giant, who had killed his father and stolen all that was his. So one day, Jack climbed the beanstalk again, in new clothes with a hat pulled down low, so that he looked a little different. After the long walk to the castle, Jack again saw the Giant's wife sitting outside.

"May I stay here for the night, I have lost my way?" he asked.

"No!" she cried, "I have been kind before to a boy who stole my magic hen. The Giant was horribly angry!"

But Jack managed to persuade the woman, and she took him into the kitchen and gave him some bread and cheese.

Suddenly, he heard the terrible roar:

"FEE, FIE, FO, FUM! I SMELL THE BLOOD OF AN ENGLISHMAN! BE HE ALIVE OR BE HE DEAD, I'LL GRIND HIS BONES TO MAKE MY BREAD!"

Quickly, the fearful wife hid Jack in the cupboard, and in stamped the Giant.

After eating his huge meal, he called for his wife to bring him his gold and silver.

Peeping through the keyhole, Jack could not believe how much money was on the table. Carefully, the Giant counted it and tied it into bags. Then he was tired and began to snore.

Jack crept to the table, grabbed the bags and ran out of the castle. After clambering down the beanstalk again, he filled his mother's arms with the bags of precious coins, until she could not hold any more. How good life was!

His mother had begged him not to climb the beanstalk again, but Jack was determined to fool the Giant once more. This time he dressed in rags and tied a cloth around his head, so that the wife would not recognize him. Then he began to climb.

It was a long climb to the top, and then a hot, tiring walk to the castle. Outside was the Giant's wife, and he asked her for some water.

"Never!" she cried, "My husband has treated me so badly since a stranger took all his money!"

But Jack looked so tired and thirsty that she took pity on him and took him to the kitchen. As he finished his drink, again he heard the deafening yell:

"FEE, FIE, FO, FUM! I SMELL THE BLOOD OF AN ENGLISHMAN! BE HE ALIVE OR BE HE DEAD, I'LL GRIND HIS BONES TO MAKE MY BREAD!"

"Quickly!" hissed the wife, and she pushed Jack into the huge copper pot she used for washing the Giant's clothes.

When the Giant stomped into the room, he was sure
there was a human hiding there. He thudded around the
kitchen, throwing open doors and kicking over buckets.
But he did not find Jack.

After eating his great meal, the Giant shouted, "Fetch me my harp!"

As Jack peered out from under the lid of the copper, he saw the wife
bring in a fine golden harp.

"Play!" commanded the Giant. And the harp began to play beautiful
and enchanting music, even though nobody touched its strings.

Jack marvelled at the sound and waited for the Giant to get sleepy.

Soon, the Giant's eyes closed and his head lolled back.
Jack crept out of the copper and slipped over to the table.
But as soon as he touched the golden harp, it
shrieked "Master!" in a loud voice.

Jack was terrified, but he was a brave boy and grabbed the harp, running as fast as he could out of the kitchen. Behind him he could hear the Giant knocking his chair back as he woke up and ran after him. Jack didn't look back, even though the harp shouted "Master! Master!" and the Giant was thundering close behind.

On Jack ran, until at last he came to the beanstalk and leapt onto it, with the harp under his arm.

Down he climbed, down from leaf to leaf,
and above him he could hear the Giant climbing too.

Jack jumped the last few feet and grabbed the axe from
the woodpile. He struck at the beanstalk once, twice, three
times. At last, the beanstalk toppled over and with it the
Giant, who landed on his huge head and died at once.

With the beanstalk gone, Jack could
never go back to the castle again,
but he did not mind. He had saved
the most precious treasures that
belonged to his father.
The Giant's wife could live
in peace, without fear of
her bullying husband.

At last, Jack could tell his mother all about
his adventures. And of course, they lived happily
ever after.